OY VEY!
LIFE IN A SHOE

by Bonnie Grubman

illustrations by Dave Mottram

APPLES & HONEY PRESS

Springfield NJ · Jerusalem

Mrs. Greenbaum lived in a shoe,
with her thirteen kids and her husband Lou.

Redhead brothers Ted and Fred,
hogged the covers and the bed.

Josh and Jake
collected rocks.

Abe and Gabe wore
clashing socks.

Sam was small and not like Zack,
but not too small to tag him back.

Side by side were
Len and Ben;
they were the twins
(numbers) nine and ten.

All around and in
between
were Dean and Dave
and sweet Maxine.

The lovely shoe was full of noise,
with jumping, yelling, happy boys.
Singing, laughing, joking too,
and a baby playing peek-a-boo.

But the husband kvetched from day to night,
"Oy vey, it's loud and much too tight.
I'm sick of looking at this mess,
and a grump I am, I must confess."
"Then go to the rabbi," said his wife.
"He'll help you find some peace in life."

"My home is shrill
and small," Lou sighed.
"From heel to toe we're
squished," he cried.
"Twelve good boys and a baby too;
with a snoring wife, what's a man to do?"

The rabbi spoke when he heard
Lou's plea.
"Take home two chickens
and listen to me.
Ask me no questions
and do as I say.
I know what I'm doing,
now be on your way."

The days and weeks were worse than before . . .

So Lou went back to the rabbi's door.
"Rabbi," he said. "What should I do?
The chickens are flapping and pecking us too."

The rabbi spoke when he heard Lou's plea.
"Take home three goats and listen to me.
Ask me no questions and do as I say.
You don't need to worry. Now be on your way."

Lou was befuddled but did what he said.
Lou brought in the goats and
plopped into bed.
The snoring was bad but
in sync with the clucking,
and hard on the ears with
the baahing and bucking.

The children were yelling; "They're ruining our stuff.
Take them away; enough is enough!"

The days that followed were worse than before . . .

So Lou went back to the rabbi's door.
"Rabbi," he begged. "What should I do?
We're *meshugga*," he said. "The place is a zoo."

The rabbi spoke when he heard Lou's plea.
"Take home two geese and listen to me.
Ask me no questions and do as I say.
Things will improve. Now be on your way."

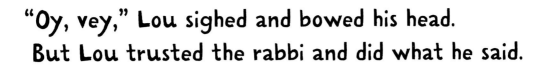

"Oy, vey," Lou sighed and bowed his head.
But Lou trusted the rabbi and did what he said.

The laughing, the singing,
the fighting, the crying
was nothing compared to the
poultry gone flying.

Life in the shoe was worse than before,
so Lou went back to the rabbi's door.

"Rabbi," Lou sobbed. "What should I do?
We've been chasing goats the whole night through.

My nerves are shot and the shoe is stinking.
Rabbi or not, what were you thinking?"

The rabbi smiled when he heard Lou's plea.
"I know what I'm doing. I promise, you'll see.

Ask me no questions and do as I say.
Your troubles will change for the better today.
Take all the animals out of the shoe.
They don't belong inside there with you."

"For joy!" Lou cheered, for thrilled he was,
and thanked the rabbi like everyone does.

He led the animals into their stalls . . .
and went back home and kissed the walls.
No more honking, no more clucking.
No more feathers, no more bucking.

No more goats to chew on toys.
No more animals making noise.
Just . . .

Singing and laughing, kvelling too,
and a baby playing peek-a-boo.
Yelling, jumping, a snoring wife;
with love in the shoe it's a bustling life!

Greetings folktale lovers,

In the beginning of the story it is fair to say that Lou Greenbaum was a grump and very unhappy with his situation. By the end of the tale Lou was a new man. He stopped complaining and thought his life was wonderful. (Snoring and all.) Hmm... Life in the shoe didn't change, but something did.

- What do you suppose happened? What changed?
- Pretend you have six little cousins who have two dogs and four hamsters. Now pretend they are staying with you for the whole summer. How do you think you would feel about sharing your room with them?
- In the story, Lou reaches out to the rabbi for help. If you ever needed advice, who would you reach out to?

It has been such fun to combine the story of *The Old Woman Who Lived In a Shoe* with the Jewish folktale about an overcrowded family. Hooray for stories that continue to teach us important life lessons and good values! I hope this one serves as a reminder that more often than not, attitude is everything.

Peace in your heart,

Bonnie

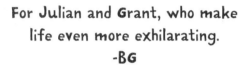
For Julian and Grant, who make life even more exhilarating.
-BG

To Sonya and Sara, who keep our shoe full of joy.
-DM

Apples & Honey Press
An imprint of Behrman House and Gefen Publishing House
Behrman House, 11 Edison Place, Springfield, New Jersey 07081
Gefen Publishing House Ltd., 6 Hatzvi Street, Jerusalem, 94386, Israel
www.applesandhoneypress.com

Text copyright ©2016 Bonnie Grubman. Illustrations copyright ©2016 Apples and Honey Press.
Edited by Ann D. Koffsky and Dena Neusner. Design by David Neuhaus/NeuStudio

ISBN 978-1-68115-515-9

Library of Congress Cataloging-in-Publication Data

Names: Grubman, Bonnie, author. | Mottram, Dave, illustrator.
Title: Oy vey! life in a shoe / by Bonnie Grubman] ; illustrations by Dave Mottram.
Description: Springfield, New Jersey : Apples & Honey Press, [2016] |
  Summary: "A retelling of a classic Jewish Folktale paired with the old woman in a shoe. The tale reminds us that sometimes things have to go from bad to worse before they can get better." Provided by publisher.
Identifiers: LCCN 2015026614 | ISBN 9781681155159
Subjects: | CYAC: Stories in rhyme. | Jews--Fiction. | Home--Fiction. |
  Families--Fiction.
Classification: LCC PZ8.3.G91915 Oy 2016 | DDC [E]--dc23 LC record available at http://lccn.loc.gov/2015026614
Printed in China
081626K1/B0885/A5